AF448228

Notes / Ex

EROTIC TALES FROM INDIA

1
Vocabulary of Indian Words

angithee: Small portable open flame fireplace of clay

bhabhi: Elder bother's wife

bhagnasa: Clitoris

bhang: An edible form of cannabis used with food and drink since ancient time in India; its intoxication is different from alcohol

belan: Thin rolling pin

bhosdi: Loosen vagina due to excessive use

boor: Same as *choot*, specially well grown up

charpoy: Indian small size portable bed, cort

chitrini: Art-woman whose *choot* is soft, raised and round

chudai: Fucking, Intercourse, Coitus

choot: Cunt, Vulva, Vagina of a woman

das: Male servant generally in service of a master but occasionally in service of lady too.

dasi: Personal girl attendant of a rich woman who confides in her

devar: Husband's younger brother

divan: Narrow recliner

duti or *kutinee*: A go between woman who arranges liaison between woman and man

faank: Labia lips

fuddi: Vagina of a woman, virgin or not fully opened up

gaand: Anus

gadda: Mattress that can be rolled up

guda: Area between anus and vagina opening

hastini: Elephant -woman, loves prolonged *chudai*

jovan: Woman breast with mounds
kama-rus: Semen
kama-salila: Water (juice) from vagina
kama-sila: G-spot
kesar kyari: Pubic hair
lund: Penis of grown up man, Member of man
laura: Penis of rather bigger dimension and thickness
mausi; Sister of mother
nanad or *nanadi*: Husband's sister
padmini: Lotus women whose *choot* is like an open lotus bud ;
       a category of women
rajai: Comforter
saali: Wife's sister
saree: A traditional dress worn by Indian woman
sasural: Wife's parents home
shankhini: Conch-woman subject to enormous passion
tawa: Griddle or flat-plate pan
vazir: Authority next to the king, chief minister

I. ROYAL INTRIGUE

1

WHY IT IS DARKER?

Once upon a time there was a kingdom and Akbar was the king and Birbal was the prime minister. Birbal was the wisest person in the kingdom with an aptitude to solve craziest problems posed by the king from time to time. The tales have no historic relevance to the Moghul Emperor. The tales and jokes on Akbar-Birbal are very common in folklore of India to enjoy the tit-wits of the duo. There were many ministers who were jealous of Birbal. The used to instigate the King to make all sorts of crazy enquiries failing which he would meet the punishment.

One day Akbar called Birbal and asked "Birbal tell me why womens' *boor* - the inner thigh part is darker than the color of her body. If you fail to answer within a week, you will be sacked as the prime minister. Birbal was in trouble as he did not know the answer. He was worried. After few days his wife enquired "What is the matter I see your face is distressed these days? Birbal told his wife what the king has asked him to answer. His wife laughed heartily "Do not worry tell your king that my wife will come at the end of the week and answer your question.

At the appointed hour, Birbal's wife came to the court of the king. All were anxiously waiting for the answer.

She slapped very hard on the face of the king. Every one was stunned. King's face became red in anger. Birbal was shaking. Before any thing further could happen, she replied very calmly "You see by hitting once your face became dark, think how many hits this has to endure day in and day out". Without naming it she pointed to her *boor.*

King was pleased with the answer and awarded her with a diamond necklace.

In another episode, the court musician who was a confidant of Birbal was obsessed with *choochis* of the queen. They were big, full round shaped protruding out with visible pointed nipples. He expressed his lust to Birbal. Birbal asked "what will I get in compensation if I arrange you to suck them?""

The musician knew that it was not possible. He told Birbal "Whatever you wish"

Birbal "I will like to reciprocate this with your wife"

Musician readily agreed.

All affairs of the palace were under his control. He used to appoint all servants for the palace. He met the *dasi* of the queen and gave her a bottle of extract of *karej* which is a high voltage itching plant that causes unbearable constant itching on contact and asked her to put some drops inside the brasiers of the queen. Soon the itching started and grew in intensity much to the king's anxiety. The royal physician could not relieve the itch.

King consulted Birbal who revealed that a special saliva, if applied for four hours, could cure it. Birbal also added that such a saliva was in the musician's mouth.

Akbar summoned the musician. For the next four hours the musician vigorously sucked the queen's melon like *choochis*. Licking, biting, pressing, playing he got what he always desired. Queen also enjoyed every bit of it.

Since his mission was over, the musician refused to honor his promise to Birbal as he knew that Birbal could never report this matter to the emperor since Birbal was himself in it.

Birbal replied to the musician that he had suspected that this could happen so he had instructed *dasi* to put drops in the underwear of the king also.

No wonder, a soldier came running and asked the musician to accompany him because the king is having acute itching on his *lund*.

2

PRICE FOR A ROBE

Once there was a King named Mahmood. In his court, besides chiefs
and ministers there was a court jester named Bahlol who used entertain
them by his wits and verses.

One day Bahlol appeared before the King.

King enquired, 'and how are you getting on with your new and with
your old wife?'

Bahlol, not satisfied with one wife, had married again.

'I am not happy,' he answered, 'neither with the old one, nor with the new one'

The King said, 'Why can you tell me?'

Bahlol recited a verse:
By reason of my ignorance I have married two wives –
And why do you complain, O husband of two wives?
I said to myself, I shall be like a lamb between them;
I shall take my pleasure upon the *jovans* of my two sheeps,
But I have become like a ram between two female jackals,
Days follow upon days, and nights upon nights,
And their yoke bears me down during both days and nights.
If I am kind to one, the other gets vexed.
And so I cannot escape from these two furies.
If you want to live well and with a free heart,
And with your hands unclenched, then do not marry.
If you must wed, then marry one wife only:
One alone is enough to satisfy two armies.
When Mahmood heard these words he began to laugh, till he nearly
tumbled over. Then, as a proof of his kindness, he gave to Bahlol his
Golden robe, a beautiful and precious vestment.
Bahlol put that robe on and in high spirits went away in the direction
towards the dwelling of the *vazir*.
Just then Hameeda looked from the terrace of palace in that direction,
and saw him.
Hameeda was the daughter of Mahmood, and the wife of the *Vazir*.
She was endowed with a most perfect beauty; of a superb figure and
harmonious form. No one in her time surpassed her in grace and
perfection. So many charms and perfections had God lavished on her.
Heroes on seeing her filled with temptation but became humble and

submissive for fear for her husband. Those who looked steadily at her
were troubled with desires. But she was very greedy by nature specially
for golden things.
She said to her *dasi*, 'Look at Bahlol dressed in such a fine robe of
goldwork. How can I manage to get possession of that?'
Dasi replied, 'Oh, my mistress, you would not know how to get hold of
that robe from Bahlol.'
Hameeda answered, 'Yes, I have thought of a trick whereby I shall get
the robe from him.'
Dasi said 'People think that they can make fun of him, but Bahlol is a
cunning man, Do not fall into the snare which you intend setting for
him.'
But Hameeda said again, 'It must be done!'
She then sent her *dasi* to get Bahlol.
Bahlol had always avoided meeting her for fear of succumbing to the
temptation; and, apprehensive for his peace of mind.
Bahlol said to himself "If a call has been made it must be answered" and
followed *dasi.*
Hameeda welcomed him and said: 'Oh, Bahlol, I believe you came to
hear me sing.'
He replied: 'Most certainly, oh, my mistress! You have a marvelous gift
for singing.'
'I also think that after having listened to my songs, you will be pleased

to take some refreshments.'

'Yes,' said He.

Then she began to sing admirably, so as to make people who listened die

with love.

After her singing, refreshment was served; he ate, and drank

Then she said to him: 'I do not know why, but I fancy you would gladly

take off your robe, to make me a present of it.'

Bahlol answered: 'Oh, my mistress! but I have sworn to give it to her, to

whom I have done as a man does to a woman.'

She asked 'Do you know what that is?'

Bahlol began to converse with her 'Do I know it?' I, who is master in

that science?; It is I who make people copulate in love, who initiate them

in the delights a female can give; show them how one must caress a

woman, and what will excite and satisfy her.

He continued "Oh, my mistress, who should know the art of love if it is

not me?"

Hameeda was obsessed with desire to have the robe, and Bahlol was

determined not to give it up without being paid for it.

'What price do you demand?,' she asked.

To which he replied, 'To taste your inside, O apple of my eyes.'

'You know what you are asking for?' she was annoyed.

He replied calmly 'Oh, lady of mine, men undertake different

occupations according to their genius and aptitude.

One is a giver, the other is a taker; one is a seller, the other is a buyer.

I think only about love and the possession of beautiful women.

I heal those who are lovesick, and provide a solace to their thirsting
choots.'

Hameeda was surprised at his words and the sweetness of his language.

'Tell me more on this subject?' she was eager to listen.

'Certainly,' he answered and recited

"Men are divided according to their affairs and doings;
Some are always in spirits and joyful, others in tears.
There are those whose life is restless and full of misery,
While, on the contrary, others are steeped in good fortune,
Always in luck's happy way, and favored in all things.
I alone am indifferent to all such matters.
My whole ambition is in love and *chudai* with women,
No doubt nor mistake about that!
If my member is without *choot*, my state becomes frightful,
My heart then burns with a fire which cannot be quenched
Look at my erect member! There it is–admire its beauty!
It calms the heat of love and quenches the hottest fires,
By its movement in and out between your thighs.
O, my hope and my love, O, noble and generous lady,
If one time will not suffice to appease the fire,
I shall do it again, so as to give satisfaction guaranteed;
No one may reproach you, for all the world does the same.
But if you choose to decline, then send me away!
Chase me away from your presence without any fear or remorse!
But, God sake, forgive me and do not reproach me.
While I am here let your words be kind and forgiving.
Let them not fall upon me like a sword, keen and cuffing!
Let me come to you and do not repel me.
Let me come to you like one that brings drink to the thirsty;
Hasten and let my hungry eyes look at your *jovan*.
Do not withhold from me love's joys, and do not be bashful,
Give yourself up to me–I shall never cause you trouble,

I shall always remain as I am, and you as you are,
Know that I am the servant, and you are the mistress ever.
Then shall our love be veiled? It shall be hidden for all time,
For I shall keep it a secret and I shall be mute and muzzled.
It is by God's will that everything happens,
And he has filled me with love towards you."
While Hameeda was listening she looked at the *lund* of Bahlol, which
stood erect like a column between his thighs.
She was over possessed. She felt unsure: 'shall I give myself to him,'
or 'shall I not.'
During this uncertainty she felt a yearning for pleasure deep within her
choot; and moisture started leaking out from her natural parts, the
forerunner of pleasure. She then no longer combated her desire to
cohabit with him, and reassured herself by the thought:
'How does it matter if he taste my *choot* once to get that precious robe?
He promises to keep it secret and even if he divulges no one will believe
his words.'
She asked him to divest himself of his robe and to come into her room,
 but Bahlol replied:
'I shall not undress till I have fulfilled my desire, O apple of my eyes'.
Hameeda then rose, trembling with excitement for what was to follow;
she undid her *saree*, and left the room.
Bahlol followed her thinking: 'Am I really awake or is this a dream?'
He walked behind her till she entered her chamber. She threw

herself on a couch of silk, which was rounded on the top like a vault,
lifted up her petticoat over her thighs, trembling all over, and all the
beauty which God had given her was in Bahlol's arms.
Bahlol examined her belly, round like an elegant cupola';
his eyes dwelt upon a navel which was like a pearl in a golden cup;
and descending lower down there was a beautiful piece of nature's
workmanship. The whiteness and shape of her thighs surprised him.
He took Hameeda in a passionate embrace, and soon saw the animation
leave her face; she seemed almost unconscious. Holding Bahlol's *lund* in
her hands, she excited and fired Bahlol more and more by running her
closed fist on it..
Bahlol said to her: 'Why do I see you so troubled?'
She answered: 'O my God, I am like a mare in heat, and you continue to
excite me still more with your words, and what words! They would set
any woman on fire, even if she was the purest creature in the world. You
succumbed me by your talk and your verses.'
Bahlol asked: 'Am I then not like your husband?'
'Much bigger than him' she said,
She continued "A woman gets heat on account of the man, as a mare on
account of the horse, whether the man be the husband or not; however, the mare gets lusty only at certain periods of the year, and only
then receives the stallion, while a woman can always be made
rampant by words of love. Both these dispositions have met

within me,

and, as my husband is absent, make haste, for he will soon be back'

Bahlol replied. 'Oh, my mistress, my loins hurt me and prevent me

mounting upon you. You take the man's position, and then take my robe

and let me depart.'

He laid himself down in the position that a woman takes to receive a

man; his *lund* was standing up like a column.

Hameeda threw herself upon Bahlol, took his member between her

hands and began to look at it.

She was astonished at its size, strength and firmness, and exclaimed

looking at the *lund*: 'Here this is the ruin of all women and the cause of

many troubles. O Bahlol! I never saw a more beautiful dart than yours!'

Still she continued keeping hold of it, and rubbed its bead against the

lips of her *choot* till the latter seemed to say: 'O dearest one, come into

me.'

Then Bahlol inserted his member into the cave of the *vazir's* wife.

She, settled down upon his shaft, and allowed it to penetrate entirely into

her furnace till nothing more could be seen of it, not the slightest trace.

She said: 'How lascivious has God made woman, and how indefatigable

after her pleasures.'

She then gave herself up to an up-and-down dance, moving

her bottom
like a riddle; to the right and left, forward and backward;
never was there such a dance she had experienced..
The king's daughter continued her ride upon Bahlol's member till the
moment of enjoyment arrived.
The attraction of *choot* seemed to pump the *lund* as though by suction:
just as an infant sucks the teat of the mother.
The acme of enjoyment came to both simultaneously, and each took the
pleasure with avidity.
Hameeda, then, seized the shaft in order to withdraw it, and slowly,
slowly she made it to come out, saying:
'This is the deed of a vigorous man.'
Then she dried the *lund* and her own *choot* with a silken kerchief and
 rose from above Bahlol.
Bahlol also got up and prepared to depart,
but she said, 'And the robe?'
He answered, 'Why, O mistress! You have been riding me, and still
want a present?'
'But,' said she, 'did you not tell me that you could not mount me on
account of the pains in your loins?'
'It matters but little,' said Bahlol. 'The first time it was your turn, now
let the second be mine, and the price for it will be the robe, and then I
will go away.'
Hameeda thought to herself, 'Since he had it, let him have it one more
time, after that he will go away'.

So she laid herself down, but Bahlol said, 'I shall not lie with you unless
you undress entirely.'

Then she took down her petticoat, her blouse and bra which were
already opened. She was fully naked.

Bahlol fell into an ecstasy on seeing the beauty and perfection of her
form. He looked at her magnificent thighs and rebounding navel, at her
belly vaulted like an arch, her plump breasts standing out like hyacinths.

Her neck was like a gazelle's, the opening of her mouth like a ing, her
lips fresh and red like a gory sabre. Her teeth might have been aken for
pearls and her cheeks for roses. Her eyes were black and well lit, and
her eyebrows of ebony resembled the rounded flourish traced by the
hand of an artist. Her face was like the full moon in the night.

Bahlol began to embrace her, to suck her lips and to kiss her full
rounded mounds; he drew her fresh saliva and bit her thighs.

So he went on till she could scarcely stammer, and her eyes became
veiled. Then he kissed her *choot*, and she moved neither hand nor foot.

He looked lovingly upon the secret parts of Hameeda, beautiful enough
to attract all eyes with their red center..

Bahlol exclaimed, 'Oh, the temptation of man!' and still he bit her and
kissed her till her desire was roused to its full pitch. Her sighs came

quicker.

Grasping his member with her hand she made it disappear in her cave.

Then it was he who moved hard, and she who responded hotly, This

went on till the overwhelming pleasure simultaneously calmed their

fervor.

Bahlol got off her, dried his pestle and her mortar, and prepared to leave.

But Hameeda asked, 'Where is the robe? You mock me, O Bahlol.'

He answered, 'O my mistress, I shall only part with it for a

consideration. You have had your dues and I had mine. The first time

was for you, the second time was for me; now the third time shall be for

the robe.'

This said. he took the robe off, folded it, and put it in Hameeda's hands,

who, having risen, lay down again on the couch and said,

'Do what you like!'

Forthwith Bahlol threw himself upon her, and with one push completely

buried his *lund* in her thriving *choot*;

then he began to work as with a hammer, and she to move her bottom to

receive the blow, until both again did flow over at the same time.

Then he rose from her side, left his robe, and went away.

Dasi said to Hameeda, 'O my mistress, is it not as I have told you?

Bahlol is a bad man, and you could not get the better of him.

People consider him as a subject of mockery, but he is the one who makes fun of them. Why would you not believe me?'

Hameeda turned to her and said, 'Do not tire me with your remarks.

Whatever had to happen is done. On the opening of each *choot* is inscribed the name of the man who is to enter it, right or wrong, for love or for hatred. If Bahlol's name had not been inscribed on my *choot,* he would never have got into it, even if he had offered me the entire universe. Look at the robe I have'

As they were thus talking there was a knock at the door.

Dasi asked 'who is there?',

In answer the voice of Bahlol said 'It is I.'

Hameeda, in doubt as to what the jester now wanted, got frightened. *Dasi* asked Bahlol as to what he wanted, and got back a reply, 'Give me a little water.'

She opened the door with a ornamental cup in her hand full of water.

Bahlol drank, and then let the cup slip out of his hands.

The cup was broken. *Dasi* shut the door upon Bahlol, who sat himself down on the threshold.

He remained seated there till *vazir*, the Hameeda's husband came home.

Seeing the jester sitting by the door, Vizir, asked 'Why do I see you here, O Bahlol?'

Bahlol calmly answered, 'O my lord, I was passing through the street when I overcame with a great thirst. A *dasi* brought me a cup of water.

The cup slipped from my hands and got broken. Then our lady of the palace took my robe, which the king had given to me, as indemnification.'

Hameeda came out at this moment and her husband asked her whether it

was true that she had taken the robe in payment for the cup.

Hameeda then shouted, clasping her hands together, 'What is this, O

Bahlol?'

He answered, 'I have spoken to your husband in the language of my

folly; you can talk to him, in the language of your wisdom as to what has

happened .'

Hameeda was enraptured with the cunning he had displayed. She could

not say any thing.

Vazir announced 'Let him have his robe back.'

Hameeda gave back Bahlol his robe, and he departed.

II INSATIABLE DESIRE

1

WOMAN WANDERING NAKED

There is a tale that relates to Koka Pandit. Koka Pandit is the adopted name of Kokkoka who is the author *Rati Rahasya,* popularly known as *koka Shastra,* an 11th century treatise on sex in India. Kokkoka himself physically engaged in the arts of love, and therefore was able to give a more extensive study with his personal endeavors. The tale account is that

there was a woman who was burning with lust. She had coitus with many men who claimed to satisfy her. However, she could not find no one to satisfy her inordinate desires. In frustration she threw off her clothes and swore that she would wander naked until she met her match.

People looked at her as she was endowed with a superb figure and
harmonious form. They filled with temptation for her but, became
humble knowing her reputation. In such a state, the police caught hold
of her and brought to the court of a king for indecent exposure. King
asked her as to why she came naked in front of so many men around in
the court. She glanced around insolently at the crowd of courtiers and
declared that there was not a man in the court. The king and all courtiers
gone abashed. Koka Pandit who was attending to the king approached
him with folded hands and asked for the royal permission to take care of
this matter. He then led her to his home and worked so persuasively so well that fainting from fatigue and repeated orgasms she cried for quarter. There upon the virile Pandit inserted gold pins into her arms and legs. Leading her before the king, made her to confess her defeat. She solemnly veiled herself in his presence.

King was, as might be expected, anxious to learn how victory had been won and commanded Koka Pandit to tell his tale and to add much useful knowledge on the subject of coition.

Based on this account of the tale the following story has been developed
including assigning the name Manjari to that woman.

Pandit Koka brought Manjari home. Manjari was a full bodied woman
She had thick hips, a rounded backside, large breasts and a non-narrow waistline. She was not overweight.

The household of Pandit Koka was full of maid servants- *dasis* of all categories with whom he enjoyed. Pandit in Sanskrit means scholarly person. Koka was master in the art of love making. His wife was of *Padmini* category- a very beautiful woman of lean physique. Her skin was so transparent that blue veins of her neck were visible through her milky white skin. She was very tender. She used to copulate once in a month on full moon night with a *dasi* in attendance since she could not sustain the assaults of her husband and the *dasi* had to rescue her with participating in full blown *chudai*. She used to enjoy watching them in various kinds of love acts.

After bringing Manjari home, first thing Pandit did was to assign her an exclusive chamber and place a *dasi* to her service. Her name was Leelavati. She herself was a *Padmini* woman- tall with round hips, full fleshy thighs, raised bust and narrow waist. There was no question of a wardrobe since Manjari was naked. Leelavati took care of food and other needs. Before retiring, Leelavati offered to give Manjari a massage.

First Night of Pleasure- *Choot* Massage
Leelavati put some incense in the oil of the lamp and made the light very
dim. The chamber was filled with sensual aroma. She laid of soft
blanket
on the bed with comfortable pillows. On *angithee* she placed the metal
bowl of mustered oil for warming up and added some herbs into it. She
 took
off all her clothes. Her perfect body was shining. Majari found her so
desirable that she Took her in arms and kissed. Leelavati did not resist
but requested to finish with her massage   She led Manjari to bed and

made her to lie dowm. She sat down cross legged towards the legs of
Manjari. Leelavati invited Manjari to lie face down. She poured the
warmed oil on her back which was so smooth to touch. she started with
long, smooth full-palm strokes up her back and down her arms. She
swirled her hands around lightly in an unpredictable, non-linear way
over the whole body. Wherever she found a tight place, spent some
time making repetitive, deeper movements over it, slowly sink nto it
with a few firm fingers or a gentle elbow. For 10-15 minutes she
massaged her back, neck, arms, hands, glutes, thighs, calves, and feet.
Leelavati felt that Manjari was absorbed into massage, she slowly led
her to turn over to face up. She continued massaging her belly and
thighs, and poured warm oil to her bally button which Manjari
immensely liked.
Then slowly she moved to massage her breast tissue, stroking along the
outside toward the nipples with her thumbs and fingers. Rubbed through
the knots in the breast for a bit to promote blood flow and relaxation.
Next her hands moved to thighs. She made long strokes up her inner
thigh toward the *choot*, Her hands were in the creases of her hips and

feeling around for those grainy, knotted spots which she was opening up

by making small circles.

Leelavat noticed that as her hands moved towards the *choot*, Manjari

was raising her buttocks. At this point Manjari was for her *choot*

massage.

As soon as Leelavati placed hands on both her thighs Manjari raised her

genital. It had opened up and was swollen with excessive use.

Next, Leelavati placed a flat palm of one hand over her *choot* and the

other hand over her heart and stayed in that position.

The next half an hour were the moments of ecstasy:

Leelavati placed one hand (completely open/outstretched) over her

entire *choot*. Then, placed the other hand over top of the first. Pressing

 into her genital she made slow circles in a clockwise and then counter-

clockwise direction for one minute each.

Leelavati opened up Manjari's legs and came between her legs. She put

her palm at the base of Manjari's *choot* with your fingers pointed up.

She moved up from the vagina up to the belly stroking her opening

without direct stimulation of her *bhagnasa*. She did the same using

palm of other hand. She repeated this for few minutes.

Leelavati brought the pads of her thumbs down to her *guda* (the area

between her *gaand* and the *choot* opening) and applied the pressure.

This is a most vulnerable spot..

Leelavati widely placed her thumbs and fingers on opposite sides of the
bhagnasa mound. Lightly squeezed together to gather the flesh, give it a
very light tug and rock it from side to side. It's similar to how someone
would pinch someone's skin, except with much wider finger placement
and much less strength.

Using the pad of her ring finger, Leelavati gently stroked the inside
groove of the outer *faank* – one side at a time, Did this for 30-60
seconds on either side, then switched.

Delicately clip her inner *faank* with her thumbs and forefingers. These
were the lips that look like two rose petals jutting out near her vaginal
opening. Gave them a soft stretch by tugging them with her fingers. Did
each a pull for five seconds, then released and repeated.

Leelavati traced a deeper pressure line around the outside of her *choot*
by using the pads of your thumbs, traced slow lines from close to her
guda, up and around her *choot*, about an inch away from her outer
faanks, and massaged a curved line up, past her *bhagnasa*, and finishing
the line to her *keasar kyari*.

By this time Manjari had raise up her *choot* which had widely opened
up. Leelavati poured a lot of warm oil into the opening till it filled up.

It felt very comforting to Manjari.

Leelavati placed the ring at the opening of her *choot*, not entirely inside

but only enough so that Manjari could feel it sitting there. The purpose

was for her to feel the invitation and evoke the idea of penetration in her

mind. Manjari was not use to it, Her *choot* was accustomed to high

strokes.She was highly aroused. She pulled Leelavati over her.

Leelavati was aroused as well. She was bisexual. She pressured her

choot on the *choot* of Manjari. Simultaneously, she moved her finger

further about 2 in. to touch the *kama-sila* – the spongey tissue on the

anterior (belly side) wall of the *choot*. With a, She dragged the tip of

slightly curled finger from the far end of the *kama-sila* to the opening

applying a pressure as brushing forward, and relaxed on the return

stroke, but always maintaining contact. Manjari more use to deep

penetration could not hold this *kamsila* stimulation and in few minutes

her *choot* started pulsating,

She held Leelavati in firm grip and moaned from *kama-sila* organisms.

Leelavati did not leave her. She kept her *choot* interlockedwith her's

giving friction till she also calmed down. Manjari slept with her arms

around Leelavati.

Second Night of Pleasure- Cunnilingus

Next night was full moon night when Koka Pandit had to be with his
wife but Manjari was not concerned since Leelavati was taking her good
care. Manjari had started liking this slim but well proportioned girl. For
next night Leelavati suggested a hot massage. Leelavati again took off
all her clothes as she made Manjari to lie down on her back. Opening up
Manjari's leg, she again sat down cross legged in-between with her open
choot to her sight. She made round pads of cotton similar to flat bread
and put them on *tawa*. When those became hot, she picked up one and
felt on her palm to see that has right temperature. Then she placed that
 pad on the *choot* of Manjari covering it fully up. She applied a good
pressure from her palm from over the pad and kept like that for a minute
and then rotated the pad over the *choot.* With pressure the passage was
opened and the clitoris and surrounding are enjoyed the heat of the pad.
This was very soothing to vagina which had some swelling. Then she
put that pad back on *tawa* and picked up the other one and did the same
thing. She alternated between the pads for a while till she felt the *choot*
became reddish with good blood circulation.
At last she left one pad covering her *choot.* She picked up the other pad

from *tawa* when it was very hot. She rapped that up on a *belan* and

slowly started inserting the cotton-rapped belan inside her *choot* cavity.

Her *choot* was deep. the entire *belan* went inside. She left it like this for

a minute. Majari was full; she felt a distinct warmness all inside her.

She almost dozed off only to come to senses when Leelavati started

rotating the *belan* slowly. Manjari felt she might explode.

As Leelavati slowly pulled out the *belan*, her last assault came. She bent

and put her mouth on her waiting *choot.* Her lips were moving up and

down, making clockwise circles, counterclockwise circles, tongue

touching side to side, tip of tongue pulsating in one spot. and sucking

around around the *kama-sila.* Manjari was over joyed. As soon as her

teeth touched the clit. Manjari cried with excitement and placed her hand

on over the head and pressed Leevati's mouth with all force within her

choot and lifted her buttock.

Third Night of Pleasure- Partial Penetration

It was a day of fun at Koka Pandit house; one day in a week friends met.

When Manjari entered Koka Pandit's main hall, the atmosphere was

very erotic, Women of the house were enjoying gossiping each other.

Most of them were half naked. Friends of inner circle of Koka Pandit

were present. After feasting they used to have some kind of
appy hour.
To night, a curtain was drawn in the middle of the hall. There
as a gap
of about one foot between the bottom of the curtain and the
oor. All
women went to the other side of the curtain. All of them
emoved any
jewelry they were putting on. All of them got naked. The lied
own
next to each other. From the other side, up to their thighs were
isible.
One by one a man had to go and recognize as many as he
ould looking
at how much was visible He could not bend to see their faces
or could
touch them but could ask them to open their legs, turn out
which
invariably they asked for. The winning person had the choice
f picking
up the woman of his liking for that night. It was a bad luck for
ther
men and women for that week.
The winning man was the Chief of Police of the King. He
icked up
Manjari. Ever since he saw her naked in the court he felt
ttracted to her
and his *lund* became tense.
Both of them were led to the chamber of Manjari. Other
ispersed.
The police chief was warmed up with the play. Manjari was
lways a
willing partner. Chief was a strongly built person. He lifted
Manjari
laid across the bed. She took off all his clothes. She was very

apprehensive. She took hold of his *lund* . She was greatly disappointed.

It was solidly erect and has a good girth but was short hardly capable of

filling up her cunt one-half. However, she was on fire and wanted to

have some thing inside her. Chief remained standing, Slowly lifted her

legs up, one at a time, and rested her ankles on his shoulders. Her hips

moved up into the air. He supported by cupping your hips b one . He

grabbed both of her ankles in another hand. He inserted pillows under

her hips to help get at a better angle. He penetrated from the top as

though drilling vertically. He started plunging into her. Her position

being inclined, his shaft was not entering directly into the passage but

was hitting the spongy spot of the *choot* wall- the *kama-sila*. Each time

his *lund* drowned in, it impacted thr *kamsila* sending a sensation through

her. He started pumping hard. She was overtaken with excitement and

had started making sound. The shunting continued. Now he was pulling

out completely and plunging with force. One time it hit her *bhagnasa*

and all through hit her *kamnasa.* She could not sustain. She made a loud

sound and her *choot* released *kama-rus.*

It did not take much time for chief to get his vigor back. Manjari was ever ready.

This time, while lying back he asked her to slide her buttocks out of the

bed. Raised her legs up in the air. Came forward to rest legs against his

chest. Holding each thigh in each hand, he lifted her pelvis to be right at

the level of his torso, he opened tighs wide open and inserted his *lund* as

though digging into her *choot.* Having the pelvis at the same height.

maximized his depth of penetration. He again adjusted to enter at an

angle and not directly along her opening. Again he was in control and

screwed her as he liked moving from side to side and churching his *lund*

in her opening. He pulled his shaft completely out in the air and pushed

in completely in one stroke. Her buttocks moved back to the bed. He

again dragged them out and take a dive. This immensely pleased

Manjari. In the course of time she crossed her legs at the anklcs to rest

her feet against his chest. Noe he was holding her shins that gave more

leverage.

He gave a good fuck to her and succeeded in getting her discharged

while he was ejaculating. He proved that the length of the member is

not a matter in satisfying a woman. But an insatiable woman like

Manjari still had an appetite for sex.

Follow Up Nights of Confrontation
In the evening next day, Leelavati gave a traditional bath to Majari with
saffron and sandalwood water meant for a bride. Brides dress lavishly
and adore jewelry for such occasion. But for oath of Manjari, Leelavati
decorated her with flowers- garland of roses in her neck and bands of
jasmine flowers on wrists. She made her to relax on a recliner and gave
her *choot* a massage. As Manjari warmed up and started pulling
Leelavati to her top, Leelavati withdrew. She led Manjari to the
chamber of Koka Pandit. Left Majari in and left the chamber closing
the door behind.
Koka Pandit was waiting for Manjari. He received her holding both her
hands and led to the bed which was nicely decorated with rose petals
sprinkled on it. He sat down next to her and started talking very sweet
to her about her beautiful well proportioned body and how graceful she
was looking. Manjari was astonished to be treated like a bride. Koka
took her in arms and kissed her lips. He kept his lips locked on her; his
kess was amazing to her. then he moved his mouth to her robust *jovan*
and took one in his mouth. As his hand moved towards her *choot,* she

could not resist   and took hold his *lund* since she was already on fire.

She felt is of an enormous size over the clothes. Now there was no time
left for formalities. He got rid of all his clothes. While he was
undressing, she had already spread her self on the bed.
Koka did not want to give up so easily. He lied down and took Majari in
his arms and resorted to kissing on her mouth and *jovan.* Manjari was in
hold of his *lund* and trying to insert it into her *choot.* Koka continued to
kiss and suck her. He slowly moved down and put his mouth on her
opening which was leaking profusely by now. Manjari moved her head
side ways in disapproval and said "come upon, insert this"
He got up. Grabbed his *lund* in closed fist touched to the lips of her
choot but did not insert. As she moved down, he also withdrew. He was
teasing her. In frustration, she snatched the *lund* from him and
completely swallowed it and made a sound *"hoon".* He gave a few
strokes which she received with much pleasure. Then he got up. She
looked at him. He indicated her to also get up.
He made her to stand by the side of the bed. She understood, bent over
and grabbed the siding of the bed. He opened both her legs. *Choot*
mouth came up right in front. Sticky white fluid had rinsed to the inner
part of right thigh. He plunged his tool into her. Her *choot* felt filled

with his big and thick shaft. He started pumping which she responded
by moving her buttocks backward.
She was enjoying the fuck. Suddenly she felt that there was a mouth
sucking her *bhagnasa*. As she looked back, she found that Leelavati
was sitting her opened legs on the ground and giving her a good blow
job. When Koka pulled out and Leelavati sneaked in, Manjari did not
noticed absorbed in her enjoyment. Koka was watching this show with
amusement. Manjari was in climax and soon succumbed to licking
tongue.
Even as she was experiencing the pulses of release, Koka did not lose
time. He lifted her across the bed and rode over her. She was not
receptive but he was pumping her up with speed. After a while her body
started responding and started participating stroke for stroke, In the
mean time. Leelavati moved near her head and lowered her *choot* over
her mouth. There was no escape but to start licking that *choot*. While
this was going on, Manjari realized that her *choot* is being fingered
rather than fucked. She saw it was so. Leevati was lying over her in
reverse position giving her a fingering job. She wanted to get out but

her grip and temptation was too much. The act continued till mutual
release.

Again no recovery time was given to Manjari. Leelavati grabbed her
knees and opened up her *choot* to the assault made by the *lund* of Koka
who was making a swing from a rope hanging from the ceiling opposite
to the bed. He will take a swing, as he will arrive near bed, Leelavati
widened the *choot* of Manjari. The *lund* penetrated like a nail. After
some time for it was not necessary for Leelavati to intervene, Majari
herself opened up her legs as widely as she could and reclined herself
backward to receive Koka's *lund* and when it entered in her with impact
she held his buttocks to keep it inside for some more moments. When
she was showing up the sign of release, Koka stopped the swing and
while he was making the preparation of *divan* for the next act, Leelavati
went over on Manjari with padded *belan*.

Through out the night fucking continued in different postures without
allowing her time in between to recoup. In the last act when he was
emitting her *kama-rus*. he hastened the pace to discharge imself.

Manjari kept holding him for a long time. In the morning when
exhausted, she was taken to her chamber.

After washing and eating as she slept, she got up in the evening. Again
a *dasi* came, a different one thing time, more of a *Shankani* class.

 Manjari was reluctant but she was made ready like yesterday and led to
the chamber of Koka Pandit.

This time another sets of positions were waiting for her in all possible
imaginable ways. She was fucked by Koka continuously that night too
till she could not take any more. She was getting dazed.

In the morning Manjari was unable to walk. Supported on the shoulder
of a *dasi* she came to her chamber. She slept throughout the day.

In the evening Leelavati came. Manjari held her hand and started crying
'I can not take it any more".

Leelavati laughed "No you have not to. Look Koka Pandit ha sent this
saree and bangles for you. I will get you ready; he will take you to the
King as a bride".

Manjari's face became red with modesty.

A veiled woman came to see the king with Koka Pandit.

King enquired "Who is she ?"

Koka lifted the veil. The woman was standing looking down with her
face red with shyness. King was astonished to see her like this

2

WOMAN WITH A RIDDLE

Roshan was a man of charm. He was well versed in the art of love
making. He was gifted with enormous size *lund*. Women of
neighborhood fell for him; they played, laughed, jested, and met his
suggestions with great pleasure. He reveled in their kisses, their close
embraces and nibbling, and in sucking their lips, breasts, and necks. He
had intercourse with all of them. However, there was a woman named
Faraha who avoided him. Faraha was all grace with perfection. She was
gifted with all imaginable charms. Her cheeks were like roses, her
forehead like white lily, her lips like coral; she had teeth like pearls, and
breasts like pomegranates. Her mouth opened round like a ring; her
tongue seemed to be incrusted with precious gems; her eyes, black and
finely slit, and her voice has the sweetness of cuckoo.
She had a fully developed form with right mass in right place.
When she walked her hidden *choot* showed in relief like a dome or an
inverted cup. In reclining it was visible between her thighs, looking like
a kid couched on a hillock.
Roshan was in love with Faraha who was alone with her husband passed
away. It was exactly her that he wanted to possess in preference to all
others. He tried to confide and rouse her interest but she was indifferent.
Whenever Roshan hinted to Faraha of his desires, she recited

to him the
following verse,
" Among the mountain top I see a tent placed firmly,
Apparent to all eyes high up in mid-air.
But, oh! the pole that held the tent up is gone.
And like a vase without a handle it remains.
With all its cords undone, its center is sinking in,
Forming a hollow like that of a kettle".
Roshan could not make out any meaning of this verse.
Every time he expressed his passion to her, she answered him with the
same verse, which to him was void of meaning,
I could not reply, but it excited his love all the more.
Roshan inquired the meaning from all he was acquainted with but no
one could solve the riddle. Roshan came to know of a guru in a far
away place who was well versed in solving riddles. He undertook
journey and met him.
Guru listened every thing including the verse.
Guru said "She is very corpulent and a full bodied woman".
Roshan answered, 'I felt exactly same. you have described her as though
she is in front of you".
He said 'She has no husband at present.'
'This is so,' Roshan replied.
Guru further stated, 'This woman loves you to the exclusion of all other
man.'
"But she is showing no interest in me"'
Then Guru pointblank asked , 'I have a reason to believe that your *lund*
is of a small dimension, and such it cannot quench her fire; for what she

wants is a lover with a member like that of an ass. So tell me he truth
about this!'
Roshan assured him that his *lund,* was a large-sized member ull of
strength,
Guru then reassured that in that case all his problems would be resolved
because those are because of her apprehension'.
He then explained the meaning of the verse as follows:
'The "tent", firmly placed, represents the *choot* of the grand limension
which is placed well forward,
The mountains between which it tops, means in-between the highs.
The "pole" that supported it is gone means that now she is without a
husband; comparing the pole to the virile member that holds up the lips
of the *choot*; it is missing now.
A 'vase without the handle' means that she is like a pail without any
support.
'With all its cords undone, its center is sinking in,
forming a hollow like that of a kettle"
This is to say, that as a tent caves in at center without a pole, without a
lund her *choot* is caving in forming a hollow like a kettle, but he interior
is intact, in this respect meant to be that the inside of her *choot* is upright
From the words, 'it forms a hollow like that of a kettle", you may judge
how lascivious that woman is?
In her comparison; she likens her *choot* to a kettle, that is used

to
        prepare a gravy food. Listen; if the gravy food is placed in the kettle, to
        turn out well it must be stirred by means of a tool, long and solid, whilst
        the kettle is firmly steadied. It cannot be done with a small spoon; the
        cook will burn hand, owing to the shortness of the handle, and the
        dish would not be well prepared.
        Guru summarized "This verse is symbolic of this woman's nature,
        When you solicited her favor she did not decline but expressed her
        apprehension that that if your member is not like a proper tool, required
        for the preparation of good gravy food, then it will not give her
        satisfaction, and, moreover, if you do not hold her firmly close to your
        chest, enlacing her with your hands and feet, it is useless to solicit her
        favors; finally if you let her consume by her own fire, like the
        bottom of the kettle which gets burnt if the tool is not stirred upon it, you
        will not be able to fulfill her desire".
        He concluded 'You see now what prevented her from acceding to your
        wishes; she was afraid that you would not be able to quench her flame
        after having fanned it.
        Guru instructed 'Go back to her, take her this verse, and your affair will
        come to a happy coitus'.
        Returning back Roshan came to know that Faraha was unwell.

e went
to see Faraha in evening. *Dasi* opened the door for him. araha was in
her room lying on her bed. Her face was not bright as used to e.

Her face lit up as she saw Roshan.   She enquired where he ad been all
along.

Roshan held her hand and boldly asked "'Did you missed me ny lady.

Now I am here, grant me your favor. .

To this she recited her verse.

In response Roshan narrated:

"No other member is like mine?
When women taste it, they fall in love with me,
Now take it, put it in right place between the mountains.
It will be quite at home there, you will find it .
Not softening while inside, but sticking like a nail;
Take it to form a handle to your vase.
Come and examine it, and notice well,
How vigorous it is and long in its attention,
If you but want a proper tool, to use between your thighs,
Take this to stir the center of your kettle.
It will do good to you, O mistress of mine!
Your kettle be it plated will be satisfied!

As he was narrating he saw her more and more lighting up, iving way
to yawns, to stretch herself, to sigh.

When he finished the verse, his *laura* was in a state of erection nat
it became like a pillar, still lengthening.

When Faraha saw it in that condition her inertia disappered ,
she took his *laura* in her hands, and drew it towards her nighs.

Roshan said, 'O my lady! this may not be done now, you are

unwell.'
     She replied, 'Leave me alone, I am fine. I was unwell as I wa
missing
     this. Oh, my God, what a member! I never saw a finer one!
Let it
     penetrate into this delicious, plump *choot* of mine, which
makes all mad
     who hear it described; for the sake of which so many includin
you have
     been longing but have not been able to get possession.'
     He repeated, 'I shall not do it unless you are well.'
     She answered, 'If you do not enter this tender *choot* right now
     I will really get sick and die.'
     Her lips tremble, her eyes filled with tears. A general tremor
ran over
      her, her color changed.
     She lifted her *saree* , baring her thighs, the whiteness of which
made her
     flesh appear like crystal tinged with carmine.
     Roshan examined her *choot*--a white cupola with a red center,
soft and
     charming. It opened like that of a mare on the approach of a
stallion.
     At that moment she seized his *laura* and kissed it, saying, 'Oh
Goodness!
     it must penetrate into my *choot*!' and drawing closer to Rosha
she
     pulled his *laura* towards her opening.
     Roshan hesitated no longer to assist her placing it against the
entrance to
     her open *choot*.
     As soon as the head of his member touched the lips, the whole
body of
     Farah trembled with excitement.
     Sighing and sobbing, she held him pressed to her *choochis*.

Again at this moment he admired the beauty of her *choot*. It was

magnificent, its reddish center setting off its whiteness all the more.

It was round, and without any imperfection; projecting like a splendidly

curved dome over her belly.

In one word, it was a masterpiece of creation as fine as could be seen. .

And the woman who possessed this wonder had no superior in he

neighborhood as Roshan had seen all.

Seeing her then in such transports, trembling like a bird, the hroat of

which is being cut, he pushed his dart into her, entering cautiously,

thinking that she might not be able to take in the whole member. But

she moved her buttocks furiously, saying 'No, this is not enough'

Making a strong push, Roshan lodged his member completely n her,

which made her utter a painful cry, but the moment after she moved with

greater fury than before.

She cried, 'Do not miss the corners, neither high nor low, but above all

things do not neglect the center!

The center!' she repeated. 'If you feel it coming, let it go into my matrix

 so as to extinguish my fire.'

They moved alternately in and out, which was delicious. Their legs were

interlocked, their muscles unbent, and so they went on with kisses and sucking mounds until the crisis came upon simultaneously.

They then rested and took breath after this mutual conflict.

Roshan wanted to withdraw his member, but she would not consent to

this and begged him not to take it out. to which Roshan acceded.

Later she took it out herself, dried it, and replaced it in her *choot* again.

They renewed games, kissing, pressing, and moving in rhythm.

She gave him a piece of an aromatic root, which she recommended to

keep in his mouth, assuring that as long as he had it there, his member

would remain in full attention..

Then she asked him to lie down. She mounted upon him, and

taking his *laura* into her hands, she made it enter entirely into her *choot*.

Roshan was astonished at the vigor of her *choot* and at the heat emitted

from it. The depth of her cave in particular excited his admiration; it

swallowed his entire shaft and touched the gland.

No other woman had until then taken in his *laura* to its full length.

Faraha, rode over him, began to rise and descend; she kept crying out,

wept, went slower, then accelerated her movements again, ceased to

move altogether; when part of his shaft became visible she looked at it,

then took it out altogether to examine it closely, then plunged it again

until it disappeared completely. So she continued until the enjoyment overcame her again.

At last, having dismounted from him, she now laid herself down, and

asked him to get on to her. Roshan did so, and she introduced his

member entirely into her *bhosadi* as it had become.

They continued their caresses, changing their positions in turns, until

morning came on.

They took scanty rest. and continued with their fucking session. She

was hungry for so long and wanted to make over.

Roshan recalled that during that evening, night and morning, they

accomplished *chudai* over twenty times.

Farah proposed to Roshan to become her legitimate husband, in order to

stop to people talking about their affair.

Roshan, on the other hand, was only on the lookout for adultery.

III DECEPTIVE WAYS

1

PERFUMED WOMAN

Aisha and Ameera were two friends. They were married to two cousins

who lived in the same house. Aslam, the husband of Aisha had a long,

thick and hard *lund*; while the organ of Ahmad, the husband of

Ameera,

on the contrary, was soft and of insignificant size. Aisha always got up

in the morning very cheerful and smiling: On the contrary, Ameera got

up in tears and vexation. Two women used to share their intimate

moments with each other. Aisha will say 'I live in the greatest happiness.

My bed is a couch of bliss. When my husband and I are together on it, it

is the witness of our supreme pleasure; of our kisses and embraces, of

our joys and amorous sighs. When my husband's member enters into me

it stretches itself out until it touches the bottom of my cave, and it does

not take its leave until it has visited every corner, threshold, vestibule,

ceiling and center to its satisfaction . When the crisis arrives it takes its

position in the very center of you know what, which it floods with tears.

It is in this way we quench our fire and appease our passion.'

Ameera will congratulate her 'you are really the blessed one'

and will sigh to herself 'I live in the greatest grief. Our bed is a bed of

thorns, our coition is a union of fatigue and trouble, of hate and

malediction. When my husband's member enters my tunnel there is

space left open all around, and it is so short it cannot touch the bottom.

When it is in erection it is twisted all ways. Feeble and meagre, it can

scarcely ejaculate and its service cannot afford pleasure to
ny woman.

Such was the almost daily conversation that two women had
gether.

After one night of deprivation when she was still in heat, when
meera
heard from Aisha the account of her night full of fucking, she
ought in
her heart that how delightful it would be have sex with Aisha's
usband.

Her body demanded, 'It must be done, even if it be only for
nce.'

Then she waited for an opportunity. The festival of Holi came.
his is a
time when people throw color on each other even when they
o
know each other. Friends catch hold of each other and smear
olor or
paint on faces. Specially *devar* and *bhabhi* play holi in full
st. The
atmosphere is sexually charged. This allow them to touch
ach others
private parts and move beyond depending upon mutual
onsent.

Ameera's husband happened to be away on business trip. She
rabbed
the opportunity to play holi with her *devar,* Aisha's husband.
he came
in good embrace with him and had a feel of his *lund* which she
oticed
was semi-erect state. She decided to move forward. In the
vening she
made preparation to get her project carried out. She prepared a
rink
laced with *bhang* and offered to him and Aisha with munchkin

as per
   tradition.
   She perfumed herself with sweet scents and essences. When the night
   was advanced she noiselessly entered the room in which Aisha and
   her husband were sleeping, and groped her way to their bed. Finding that
   there was a free space between them, she slipped in. There was scant
   room, but each of the spouses thought it was thepressure of th other,
   and gave way a little; so she contrived to glide between them. She then
   quietly waited until Aisha was in a profound sleep.
   Then, approaching Aslam, the husband of Aisha, she brought her flesh
   in contact with his. He awoke, and smelling the perfumed odors which
   she emitted, he was in erection at once. Aslam drew Ameera towards
   him, but she whispered, 'Let me go to sleep!'
   Aslam answered, 'Be quiet, and let me do! Let children not hear
   anything!'
   Ameera pressed close up to him, so as to get Aslam farther away from
    his wife, and whispered again,
    'Do as you like, but do not awaken the children, who are clos by.'
   She took these precautions for fear so that Aisha should not wake up.
   The man, however, roused by the odor of the perfumes, drew her
   ardently towards himself. She was plump and mellow, and he

hoot

projecting. He mounted upon her and pointing to his *lund* said, 'Take this
in your hand, as usual!'

She caught it, and was astonished at its size and magnificence, then she
introduced his *lund* into her *choot*.

Aslam, however, observed that his member had been taken in entirely
which he had never been able to do with his wife.

Ameera, on her part, found that she had never received such a benefit
from her husband.

Aslam was quite surprised but was overtaken by passion to pump hard
into the receptive tunnel.

Again he worked his will upon her for a second and third time, but his
astonishment only increased. with response from the other side.

At last he got off her, and stretched himself along her side.

As soon as Ameera found that he was asleep, she slipped out, left the
room, and returned to her own.

In the morning, Aslam, on rising, said to his wife, 'Your embraces have
never seemed so sweet to me as last night, and I never breathed such
sweet perfume.'

'What embraces and what perfumes are you speaking of' asked his wife.

'I have not a particle of perfume in the house.'

She told him you might be hallucinating because of *bhang* you had.

Aslam was puzzled, but then accepted what his wife saying.

After that the copulation of Aisha and Aslam was not the same. He used
to miss the deepness that could have accommodated even more than his
penetration, and the response for his each thrust and that perfume he
exhaled. He use to get lost in the thought, forget to make strokes and
absently ejaculated.
Aisha during conversation brought this up with Ameera. Ameera
thrilled to know that Aslam liked her *chudai*. She was also feeling
a desire for getting pleasure once more. Again, a day when Ahmad was
 away from home, Ameera prepared herself with care applying the same
perfume. She went to see Aisha when Aslam was present. Aslam
immediately recognized the perfume. As Aisha and Ameera were
conversing.
Aslam was constantly looking at Ameera. Ameera was cunningly
returning back his stare with half-closed suggestive eyes. When she was
leaving, she dropped her perfumed kerchief. Aslam grabbed it. There
was a small message "tonight at midnight in my room"
As Aisha was asleep, Aslam quietly sneaked out. Amara was waiting.
This time they had pleasure to their heat content. He pumped her *lund*
as hard as he could which she received by raising her *choot* for every

stroke. She was moaning with pleasure as loudly as she wanted without
 restrain.
They had two rounds. Aslam wanted more but Ameera was scared of
Aisha waking up and begged him to go back.
Since then it became their regular routine. Whenever Ahmad went out,
Ameera will dress up with lot of perfume and night will color up
with their heart rendering *chudai*, and Ameera's loud moaning.
The conversation between Aisha and Ameera changed now. Aisha used
to complain about missing days and lack of energy in their love making.
Ameera was beaming up with joy and pleasure of life.

2

TREACHEROUS WOMAN

A rich man fell in love with a very sexy married woman of great
proportions. Her name was Faiza. She had large breast that stood straight
 up with erect nipples. She had heavy round buttocks protruding
backward. When she crossed her thighs one over the other her *choot*
stood out like the head of a calf. When she walked, this inner piece was
apparent under her clothes by its wary movement at each step.
He made advances to her, which she did not seem to take note of; he

endeavored her by rich presents, which were likewise not accepted. This
lasted for some time, when he met, a *duti-* an old go between woman,
whom he took into his confidence. In India there are many go between
women who provide their services to make liaison successful between
married man and woman.
Duti said to him, 'Surely, I shall help you with this. If she is longing for
love beside her husband she will be in your arm'
In next few days *duti* made enquiries about Faiza, from neighbors,
relatives and other *duties* in the surrounding.
She returned back to Faiza's house with flowers and cut meat basket as
he had enquired that there was a female dog in the house..
On seeing her, the dog jumped at her; but she produced the basket with
 its contents. Seeing the meat, the dog mellowed and moved her tail and
nostrils. While the animal was eating, and *duti* stroking her back, the
 mistress of the house came and was surprised to see thar the dog,
who did not allow anybody to come near the house, was so friendly
 with a stranger.
Faiza asked 'O old woman, who are you?'
Duti said very sweetly "I am your *mausi,* sister of your mother from a
distant relation. I was in the neighborhood and came to know about you,
hence came to see you".

Duti was trained in art of conversation. Faiza started conversing very

fondly with her.

When she left, Faiza asked to come again.

That opened up the door for *duti* to regularly visit Faiza.

First duti assessed whether Faiza has interest in other man,

Faiza fondly talked about a man she was in love with. Then his father

arranged the marriage with Ahmad, the present husband"

"Did you copulate?" she enquired

Faiza's face became red.

Duti "Come on, I am your *mausi*, do not hide any thing from me"

Faiza in low tone 'Yes we did"

Duti "Did you like it?"

Faiza "Yes, very much"

Duti "If you find him, will you do it again"

Faiza jumped "No, no. How is it possible I am married now.

I love my husband, Ahmad"

Duti "Okay, okay, I was just asking. but if you do it is perfectly fine.

Enjoying life does not take away your husband. You loved that person

any way,"

This way she planted the seed for extra marital in the mind of Faiza and

also understood that she could be worked with.

After that *duti*'s role started.

She first played a sympathy factor " I have a nephew. How unlucky he

is. His wife deserted him; he is heart broken Although he is a rich

person, he remains very depressed. She is trying to get him out of it.

She showed the photo of rich person to Faiza.

Faiza recognized him "I know this man. He incurred large expenses to
 gain my favor but I did not respond"
'Tell me, you did not like this man,' asked *duti*.
"I liked him but not his approach was not annoying" answere
Faiza,
Next day, *duti* told Faiza "As soon as I told him about you, h
jumped
up. He is still longing for you. Here is a gift he sent for you'
She gave her a gold necklace which she accepted on
persuasion of *duti*.
Every time *duti* met Faiza he brought a gift which Faiza
thrilled to
receive.
Duti gave her a photo and told that this she can watch only in
the
private.
When Faiza saw an enormous size *lund* in full erection, she
felt tremor
in her body and *choot* leaked out the moisture. That night sh
had heavy
chudai from Ahmad but was still longing for that big *lund*.
Duti asked for a similar photo of her so that he could he coul
keep in
private. Instead of feeling offended, she was apologic that sh
did not
 have one.
This was the time they started exchanging letters through *dut*
They were full of expressions.
" It is ready for action and does not die down;
It never sleeps, owing to the love for you.
It is sighing to enter its destination, full of vigor and life.
It will works there in action constant and splendid.
From front to back, and then from right to left."

"You are welcome, you light of my eyes!
You man of all men, who fill me with pleasure.
When you will open my thighs and kiss my belly,
And put your tool in my hand, soon it will be in the cave..
It will shake me, trill me, and fill me with bliss.
For you must not withdraw it from me;
leave it there as long as you wish ,
And this day will then be free of all sorrow".

Faiza could not wait longer 'Make haste, *mausi*, and see him before
    some thing goes wrong,'
'I will see him to day,' answered *duti*, 'you shall meet him tomorrow.'
    With this, *duti* went to the man who had made her his confidant, and
    arrange the meeting for the next day.
    Next day Faiza went to the house of *duti*, for they had agreed that the
    rendezvous should take place there. She arrived at the house waiting for
    him. She was burning with lust, her *choot* was wet with *kaam-rus*.
    But the lover did not show up. must be some important matter that had
    prevented him from keeping up the promise.
Duti looked at Faiza and found her agitated, it was apparent that she
    badly wanted *chudai*.
    Faiza getting more and more restless as time passed, eagerly enquired ,
    'Why did not he come?'
Duti replied, 'My daughter, some serious thing must have happened,
    probably making him to go out. But do not worry I will help

you under
    these circumstances.'
    Duti thought, 'At this moment, this woman eagerly needs a man. Why
    not try another young man for now. Tomorrow I am sure l wil find out
    that rich man.'
    Duti went out to search a suitable substitute. She saw a very handsome
     person.
    She approached him: 'Trust me, if I arrange a perfect beautifu lady for
    you. would you make love to her?"
    The man replied "If you are telling the truth, surely I will do and pay a
     coin you might be looking for"
    Duti took the money, and brought that man to her home and asked him
    to wait outside.
    It so happened that this young man was Ahmad, the husband of Faiza,
    which the *duti* had no knowledge of.
    Duti went inside the house first and asked Faiza "Look, I could not find your lover
    but I have brought someone else to quench your fire for now. Save your
    lover, for tomorrow.'
    Faiza agreed and then went to the window to take a look at the man
    who the *duti* had brought,
    She recognized it was her husband that *duti* had picked up.
    As her husband entered the house, she hastily veiled and went to
    meet him,
    Striking him on the face, she exclaimed, 'My God, what are

ou doing

here? I suspected you for a long time. I waited here every day
nd sent

this old woman to look for you and ask to come in. This day I
ave

caught you. The denial is of no use now.

Ahmad, believed that his wife is telling the truth, could no
utter a word.

IV SURPRISE ELEMENT

1

WEDDING AFFAIR

It was a wedding occasion, Shashi's younger brother was
getting married. She was from a rural setting where daughters and
other female relations used to arrive to participate in the
celebrations long before the event. She too arrived to her parents
home a month in advance. She was from a big family of . three
brothers two sisters. All gathered for the occasion.   So did the
children of two uncles of Shashi. Not only this, the distance
relatives accepted the invitation and their ladies arrived well ahead
of time as per extended family tradition . The house was full. There
were ten women staying in the same house as per tradition. The
environment was full of joy as expected on such an occasion. Ladies
gathered long before the wedding date to take care of various
chores, however, men used to arrive three to four days before
marriage date. Shashi's husband Sachin also arrived a week ago to
his *sasural*. He was feeling very lonely by now. Shashi and Sachin

used to do have sex every other day. Shashi very much enjoyed *chudai* too. Sachin was feeling restless. Shashi was also tipsy for not getting a dose of good fuck. In full house they could not meet in isolation. Once when they stole few moments of private meeting, Shashi flung into Sachinand started rubbing her *choot* on his *lund* from above the clothes.

Sachin expressed his love by kissing and fondling her *choochis* and said, "Shashi, my condition is very bad." If you don't do anything, then I will go mad "

Shashi responded" I am in the same condition myself. Listen, will try to do something".

But that was not an easy task. The house was big but there were so many women. They all used to be in play full mood and doing wedding chores and chatting to each other till late hours of night.   They all slept on the ground making their beds by spreading a *gadda* side by side. The beds of men were similarly laid in other rooms. Only sons-in-laws like Sachin were given *charpoy*. However, Sachin's room too had three more charpoys.

Shashi and Sachin thought of renting a room in a hotel for an afternoon and enjoy. But her absence was sure to be noticed by her sisters and *bhabhis*.

When they could not bear the urge for sex any longer, Shashi devised a plan, she suggested, "Look it is winter time, while sleeping all women cover up their body in *rajai*. I will sleep wearing a diamond ring. It will shine in the darkness. In the dead hours of the night, you sneak in the room where we sleep, recognize me by the shine of ring and get into *rajai* and do what you want"

This was a risky adventure but in their plight they were prepared to do anything.

As planned, Sachin woke up in the night on the pretext of visiting bathroom. The diamond ring was shining on the first person in the ladies sleeping room. Shashi too was awake and waiting with all eagerness. She had taken off her panty, unbuttoned her blouse and brazier hooks were opened up.

As Sachin climbed on top of her, Shashi inserted her hand his ujama and took out his *lund*. She widened her thighs and inserted s tightly erected member in her wet pulsating *choot*. She tied oth her toes over his waist. He took one *choochi* in his mouth and e other in his palm. Without wasting time he started to pump. He as sucking nipples badly and kneading the other as he was hungry or so long. His *lund* was shunting nonstop. Shashi was accepting ach stroke and on each blow raising her buttocks. She was holding er screams with great difficulty; still, she was making sound "*hoo oo*". At last, they achieved their climax. He slipped out as quietly s he had come.

The next day both were very happy and their love was nowing up through their looks towards each other. The plan had orked.

They had now devised their way. They used to have fun egularly at night. Sachin will alert her during the day so that Shashi ill be prepared by removing her undies and opening her top. He ill quickly enter into comforter and their *chudai* session will take lace with vigor from both side. Sachin loved to make surprised nannounced visits too, but Shashi was ever willing. She used to eep without panty in night'

In the morning of one such surprised visit, Sachin complained, Last night, you made a big tantrum"

Shashi, "Whaaaaaaaaaat? But I don't have that ring since esterday. I forgot to put it back on my finger after the bath esterday and later could not find in the bathroom. I enquired but no ne that I know picked it"

Sachin touched his head in disbelief "O, my God, then who as she?

Shashi" You don't even notice the difference?"

Sachin "As soon as I entered into opening, she screamed but I nuffled that by putting my hand over the mouth.

Shashi "And how did you manage to get the panty off?

Sachin " There was no panty, as in your case, you take it of ".

He continued " I was surprised that she offered resistance while opening up her legs. The tunnel felt a little tight too. But, the I presumed that it is so because you were tired with work whole day. Assuming it was you, at first, you behaved very upright and b then started participated so forcefully. My each stroke matched wit back stroke from your side.

In fact I gave up earlier but you did your work by grinding your *choot* with motion till you got release".

Shashi", I do not know who you fucked?. Who that woman is I wish it might not lead us into trouble "

Now Sachin was concerned too" Please try to find out "

Sachin was very keen to know. On getting an opportunity in the afternoon, he asked "Did you come to know anything?"

Shashi "The ring has been found. Someone left it back in the bathroom. But no one came forward '

Sachin "Thank God, but please keep an eye on everyone"

Shashi "Now control yourself, keep off for few days"

Next morning when Sachin got up he found a panty under his pillow. It had a stain the front.

There was a letter along with it.

Letter read "Recognize me. I am the one you had a night stand. I am leaving my panty. Its smell might help you to recognize me since you smelled me the other night. If you find me, then the thing which this panty covers covered is yours. If I like my thing better than your wife, then accept my challenge and don't tell your wife any thing.

As instructed, Sachin did not say any thing to Shashi. His eye were searching the one with that panty.

The next day a photo came out from under the pillow. There was a photo of buttocks tightly wrapped in *saree*.

Together with a letter "What you are looking in *saree* are waiting for you. Come and liberate them from *saree*. If you have recognized, then catch me"

Sachin was gaging buttocks of all women. Sometimes it seemed that this was Shashi's younger *bhabhi*, sometimes she seemed to be the his *saali*, who was one year older to her.

Seeing him staring women like this, Shashi asked, "What is the matter? where are your eyes wandering today ?. Are you feeling okay?

And the next day there was another photo and a letter under the pillow. Sachin was surprised that he did not see anyone coming into the room, then how the photos and letters appeared .

This time it was a front pose A fine pussy was visible under a thin layered wet *saree.* The thighs were full and the center piece was protruding. Sachin got instant erection.

Message was "Now you know me, don't you? Everything is in front of you. How much will you torture me? Don't you see me. I am in front of you "

Sachin was looking closely at the central part of all the women from over the *sarees*. He was certain that this is his *saali* who used to flirt with him.

But his decision soon disappeared. At breakfast, when his *saali* came to serve him a food item, under the table, he touched her thigh with his knee.

However, she quickly turned around and stood beside her husband.

While getting ready for bathing after the breakfast, he found a letter inside the

pocket of the pant hanging in closet leaving him astonished as to who could do all

this with such a sweep.

"My prince, I can not see your wandering any more. Even in front of you, you can not recognize your sweet heart. Let's overcome your anxiety. Let us meet at seven o'clock in the evening at this address, but do not be ferocious like that night".

The address given was of a nearby house, which belonged to one of their relatives.

In the mean time Shashi came to see Sachin and happily told him "I have managed to get consent of *bhabhi*. Let's go to movie tonight and we will have some fun ".

However Sachin retracted, "No. I have to meet my old friend today"

Sachin reached the place at appointed hour. The one who opened the door was scantly dressed but had a long veil. She was a full bodied woman with raised *choochis* and very sensuous firm buttocks. . With agesture, he made Sachin sit on the couch and handed an envelope to him.

Sachin opened it. There were photos. The first photo was of the *saree* clad buttocks that he had before. The second was of the see through pussy he got earlier. The third photo was the breast part with *saree* falling to one side, her fully developed *choochis* were trying to tear apart her blouse. Then next photo was up to the chin. Sachin felt it like something familiar. Then there was final photo- a close up of Shash's face.

Veiled woman extended her hand towards Sachin but that instant Shashi came to the room from the inside of the house.

She was shocked "What's happening?"

Sachin got up in panic. So this was the plot of these women.

Let us take story back. What Shashi told Sachin that she found back the ring in bathroom was not true. In fact when Shashi was searching for her ring, Sunita came and announced to Shashi "*Nanadi* I have to speak to you". Sunita was *Bhabhi* of Shashi's elder *Bhabhi*. She was of the same age like her elder *Bhabhi*, about five years older than Shashi. She was from a rural area. Due to hard work on farms her body was steady and well set. She was full bodied but lean and tall,and well educated too.

Taking Shashi inside a room, Sunita took out a ring "You are searching for this"

She was very agitated "You see your husband has ruined me. He forced himself on me. He covered my mouth with palm

Shashi "This all happened with mistaken identity"

Sunita "But I have been left no where. When my husband ears, I do not know what will be my fate".

Shashi fell on her feet "*Bhabhi*, please do not drag this issue urther. No body will know. I am ready to do whatever you want. f you want me to do sex you're your husband I am willing to do".

Sunita calmed down. Getting Shashi up "Let this be bygone. But one thig for sure your husband has tremendous sex drive. Do ou enjoy tremendously?".

Shashi "What can I say *Bhabhi*, I my self can not hold it nless I get the dose every other day. That's why we landed in this rouble"

Sunita "But so quickly you became ready to get laid by my usband. Do you have many extra sources to quench fire?"

Shashi "Never. I got so afraid of your anger. You were really gitated".

Sunita "Never ever you you had any one do it?"

Shashi kept quite. Sunita started laughing

Sunita "Tell me how many affairs your husband have?"

Shashi "He does not have any one except me. He loves me ery much".

Sunita "And what that he did with me?"

Shashi "It happened by mistake"

Sunita "But I think, he had sensed it that it was some one else"

Shashi "No, it is not so".

Sunita "Okay, let's play a game. If you win then I will not ursue what happened to me. but if you lose then I will enjoy him to ny heart conent, after all I have been ruined by him any way"

And that's how this whole thing was planned out by Sunita.

Sachin was fully trapped.

Shashi had never expected this and was razed with anger.

Sunita pleaded "*Bhabhi*, calm down it happens".

Shashi "How can I calm down. This man sees me naked every lay but could not recognize even one thing of mine".

Sunita "*Bhabhi*, it never occurred to him that it could be you".

Shashi "So he was so eager to fuck another woman that he ke kept every thing secret from me. Today he told me that he had to meet a friend".

Shashi started crying " He destroyed all promises he made with me"

Sachin put a hand on her shoulder but Shashi roared like a lioness "Do not touch me. I will not live with you".

Sunita, holding her hand made Shashi to sit down "Don't get swayed in emotions. Keep control on yourself. If you do not live with him, what will you do then?"

Shashi "I will do any thing but will not live with this cheat".

Sunita asked Sachin to sit down as well and asked "Do you want to say any thing?".

Sachin did not speak. He placed is palm on the arem of Shashi and started crying.

Shashi put away his palm.

Sunita "*Bhabhi,* all men are like this. But how can we blame them if some one is so eagerly offering her *choot*, how one can refuse unless he does not get erection or has renunciation.

Sunita continued " And you people are full of sex and on top of that deprived of *chudai*. *Bhabhi*, let me ask you. If some one embraces you, kisses you, fondles your *choochies* and you have been deprived of sex, will you not get ready to offer him your *choot*? See the other day I had no intention but then participated fully".

Looking at Sachin, Sunita said "Definitely you are guilty. You spoiled me and then *Bhabhi* had to apologize. You have to pay for it".

Sachin held the hand od Shashi and said with sincerity "Believe me I did not want to hurt you at all"

Sunita "This is true *Bhabhi*, he loves you very much. It is some thing else that was not cooperating with him".

Shashi " *Nanadi*, I lost the bet. He is your now".

Sunita "From my side this is a gift to you. Settle your fight with full force all night along and a couple of times taking my

me too. Till tomorrow you have all the time since I told them that
ou are coming to my village till then".

'Your game had made me so hot, I am going with my
usband who is waiting outside" saying this she closed the door
ehind and walked out.

2

FRIEND IN DEED

This is the story of two fast girl friends- Merry and Jyoti.
hey are both still close friends. In the college, Jyoti came from
oona. Her father was a senior officer in the central government and
ame on transfer. Merry and Jyoti were allotted the same room in
ormitory . From the very first day, they started getting well
gether. They have similar likings; in eating, drinking, clothes
election, movies etc. Just their language was different. Jyoti was
Marathi speaking and Merry spoke English and Hindi . But Jyoti
ad no problem speaking English. Mostly they hanged around
gether,. The pair had become famous in the college.

A third girl Pammi joined them. She was a Punjabi girl, very
air complexioned and tall. She was full bodied; not fat. She looked
exy and in reality also she was sexy. She created the sex feelings in
Merry and Jyoti too.

There was a small pond nearby in which they used to go
wimming. Pammi used to take off her under pants inside the water.
he used to swim naked under her waist. She even swam to the
roximity of swimming men. She used to get thrill out of it. In the
ater, all three used to touch each other's intimate parts. In case of
ammi, the hands of Merry and Jyoti directly touched her pussy and
he would spread her legs. They used to get very hot. This was the
xtent of sex among them, beyond that was taboo. But, in effect
Merry and Jyoti inadvertently did move forward .

Once Merry had high fever. Jyoti was comforting her with
ed pack on head. Out of pity or what, jyoti placed her lips on

Merry's lips. Merry caught hold of Jyoti's head with her left hand and kept sucking the lips. Out of habit of pool, Jyoti's hand reache between legs of Merry. Merry pulled Jyoti over her top and kept kissing each other. They kept interlocked like this for some time.

Next day they moved further. When they returned back after swimming Jyoti was breathing fast. Pammi had excited her by inserting her finger inside her panty. As soon as they entered room Jyoti caught hold of Merry and dragged her panty away. Merry als pulled down Jyoti's panty and dropped to the floor. Merry pulled the top of Jyoti over her head. Jyoti also removed the top of Merry Both of them clingged together facing each with their lips locked. They fell together on the bed in this condition. When separated the found that *choots* of both were dripping. Their *choots* were similar protruding in between thighs with juicy lips neither too big nor too small. Jyoti rode over Merry. Merry opened her legs to receive he part over her. Merry's *choot* was covered by the *choot* of Jyoti.

Jyoti took Merry's lips into her lips are started kissing makin loud sucking sound. She started rubbing her *choot* on the *choot* of Merry. By itself their *choots* interlocked; one lip of Jyoti inside the opening of Merry. THey were rubbing their *choots* and sucking lip

They were in full heat.

"*hoon hoon hoon hoon……..* ' sounds filled the room.

Their assaulting each other with force continued till they calmed down. Then they slept in each others arms.

Their friendship had acquired a new dimension. They used to enjoy each other. Even otherwise, they used to sleep in one bed together.

Graduating from college, they separated. First Jyoti got married to a manager in a private company. Then Merry got marrie to an engineer. Merry went to Jyoti's wedding. She shared her firs night experience with Merry. Her husband was great in sex.

Jyoti came to the wedding of Merry. Moe, my husband had a lot of flirting with her. The secret remained in their midst. Over th period of time both got busy in their lives and contact remained to occasional conversation.

One day Jyoti got a call from Merry "Listen Jyoti, I have a news for you. Moe is coming to your place for three weeks. His company is commission a new project there. The company had made a booking in a hotel, but then I persisted that when Jyoti is there why he should is the hotel "

Jyoti" This is a good news "

Merry" Good or bad that I do not know. But he is in your hand

Jyoti" Why don't you come too Merry It will be great fun".

मैं मजाक करती तो पलट कर वह जवाब देते तो सचिन उनको सपोर्ट करता।

मैं उनका हर ख्याल रख रही थी। सुबह की चाय से ले कर घूमने फिरने तक का।

एक हफ्ते तक तो ठीक रहा। उसके बाद मैं उनकी सुबह चाय ले कर जाती तो देखती कि उनका ण्ड खड़ा हुआ है। अच्छा खासा साइज का।

 कर मुझे घूरते हैं और अपने लण्ड पर हाथ फेरते रहते हैं।

मैं उनकी हर खुशी का खयाल रख रही थी। पर इस बाबत कुछ नहीं कर सकती थी।

ज्योति से मेरी बात होती रहती थी।

ज्योति ने पूछा ''और राजन के क्या हाल चाल हैं?''

Merry "No, I will not be able to leave at all this time. You have to handle him alone "

Merry's husband, Moe came. In two years he had not changed a bit. The same tight exercised body. He started getting very well with Rajan, my husband. Both could talk for hours.

Moe flirted with Jyoti to an extent expected in a relation between *Bhabhi* and *devar*.

When Jyoti made a double meaning joke, Moe would promptly respond and Rajan would lend a support to him.

Jyoti was taking care of Moe. From morning tea to taking him around.

It went well for a week. Then Jyoti noticed that when she would go with morning tea to his room, Moe's *lund* would be erect like a pig pole. It had big dimension as she could see. He used to be half asleep.

She used to feel very shy to get him up and used to leave the tea by his side. Moe did not mention but Rajan complained about serving cold tea when he came to know.

One more thing Jyoti noticed. Their exercise room was just in fron of the guest room. Jyoti used to exercise putting a tight polo and short. When she used to ride on treadmill, he found that Moe *lund* would be erect and he would rub it stealing the glance.

Jyoti wanted to take good care of Moe and keep him happy, but nothing she could do about this condition.

Merry and Jyoti used to talk more regularly these days.

Merry "Moe was praising you very much. He was saying how much you take care of him".

Jyoti started laughing "Was he saying some thing else?".

Merry "No, what's the matter".

Jyoti "Merry, he needs you now".

Merry also started laughing "So you noticed now. He remained without me for so many days is a miracle. Here he won't stay even for two days".

Jyoti "How can I not notice? When I go with tea in morning the snake is up with full fury. I am trying to take care of him but what can I do to this?"

Merry "How does it matter between me and you. Satisgy his hunger. Shelter that snake in your cave".

Jyoti "Wait a minute. Do you have any idea what are you talking regarding your husband?".

Merry "Are we different?"

Jyoti "Forget that. We have husbands now. Those things are not ours, they belong to them. Only they have the right on them".

Merry "Okay, the faithful one. But at least show that to him. He will discharge with your name. He has to spend two more weeks there."

Merry's words planted thoughts within me. Seeing big *lund* o Moe I used to get excited, specially on those days when Rajan discharged before releasing me.

By week end they made a camping program in a resort nearby; outside cooking, tracking and sleeping in tent.

Inside the tent, the *gadda* were spread on the ground. The order of sleeping was first Moe, then Rajan in-between and Jyoti last on the right. Every one was tired, hence slept early. As per habit, Rajan got up early in the morning and went away for walking. knew that he will not be back for an hour. Jyoti saw that Moe was wake too with his snake holding his head up. She got up pretending to be half-asleep and rubbing her eyes went out of tent to ase her bladder. Outside, she took out her panty and came in ubbling words within as though she is still sleep. She lied down ext to Moe. She inserted her hand inside pajama of Moe and olding his *lund* in her hand she spoke very softly

"O, Rajan come on now, Moe is sleeping away any way" and he lifted her night gown anove her thighs.

Without losing a minute, Moe turned over and inserted his ntire shaft in the *choot* of Jyoti in one thrust. *The* big *lund* made uch an impact that shrill came ot from Jyoti *"hoo hoo hoo hoo hoo oo*, slow down please".

Moe had forgotten the situation in excitement. He started *hudai* with a slow pace. Jyoti kept her eyes closed enjoying the uck.

But she wanted the higher pace.

She encouraged him " Yes, yes. do it, more, do it"
"

Moe was on a regular pace pumping his *lund* inside her *choot.*
"Oohooo aaaaaaaaaaaaa ooooooooooo my,
ooooooooooohooooo my"

His *lund* started shunting like a piston
"Rajaaaaaaaaaaaaaaaaaanoooooooooohhhhhhhhhhhhhhhhhhh
aaaaaaaaaa"

"Yes, Yes, more, yes,
nyeeeeeeeeRaaaaaaaaaaaaajaaaaaaaaaaaaan"

Moe *lund* was getting in fast entirely and coming out and gain plunging in

He was fucking, fucking, and fucking. She was getting fucked, fucked, and fucked.

"My daaarliiiiinggg"

"aaaaaaaaaaaaaaaaaaaaaaaaaaaaaaaaaaaaaaaaaaaaaaaaaahooooooo
oooooooooooooooooooaaaaaaaaaaaaaaaaaaaaaaaaaaaaaaaaaa
aaaaahoooooooooooooooooooooooooooooo

oomyyyyyyyyyyyyyyyyyyyydaaaaaaaaaaaaaaaaaaaaaaarrrrrrrr
iiiiiiiiiiiiiiiiiiiiiiggggggggggggggggggggggggg"

She was released

Moe started strokes to get himself released

Jyoti "Rajan do not discharge inside me"

Still she was pretending

Moe took is *lund* out and released the load that was building inside him for a long lied dotime. Then he went outside,

Jyoti opened the eyes and had a hearty laugh. Cleaning herself with gown, she lied down to her side.

Returning back to tent, Moe saw her and thought she was sleeping. He also lied down making a distance in-between.

The sleep overtook Jyoti. When she got uo, the sun was up. Rajan had returned back. Moe was making tea. He was very happy.

Looking at Jyoti, Moe said "Good morning, dear *saali*. Did you have a nice sleep?"

Till today Moe has no idea that Jyoti has knowledge of who fucked her. Rajan does not know any thing. And Jyoti did not tell even Merry about this.